I Like to Read® books, created by award-winning picture book artists as well as talented newcomers, instill confidence and the joy of reading in new readers.

We want to hear every new reader say, "I like to read!"

Visit our website for flash cards and activities:
www.holidayhouse.com/ILiketoRead
#iLTR
This book has been tested by an educational expert and determined to be a guided reading level G.

This book has been officially leveled by using the F&P Text Level Gradient™ Leveling System.

HORSE & BUGGY
PLANT A SEED!

Ethan Long

I Like to Read®

HOLIDAY HOUSE • NEW YORK

HOLIDAY HOUSE is registered in the U.S. Patent and Trademark Office.

Printed and bound in April 2020 at Tien Wah Press, Johor Bahru, Johor, Malaysia.

The artwork was created digitally.

www.holidayhouse.com

First Edition

1 3 5 7 9 10 8 6 4 2

This book has been officially leveled by using
the F&P Text Level Gradient™ Leveling System.

Library of Congress Cataloging-in-Publication Data

Names: Long, Ethan, author, illustrator.
Title: Horse & Buggy plant a seed! / Ethan Long.
Other titles: Horse and Buggy plant a seed
Description: First edition. | New York : Holiday House, [2020] | Audience:
Ages 4-8. | Audience: Grades K-1. | Summary: After Horse and his friend
Buggy plant a seed, Horse must exercise patience while waiting for it to grow.
Identifiers: LCCN 2019029200 | ISBN 9780823444984 (hardcover)
Subjects: CYAC: Gardening—Fiction. | Seeds—Fiction. | Patience—Fiction
Horses—Fiction. | Carriages and carts—Fiction.
Classification: LCC PZ7.L8453 Hor 2020 | DDC [E]—dc23
LC record available at https://lccn.loc.gov/2019029200

ISBN 978-0-8234-4498-4 (hardcover)